Days of

Volume 1

The Healer's Touch

By

Amber Schamel

Author's Note

Thank you so much for joining me on Aaliyah's journey! The journey will continue in Volume 2 in the Days of Messiah Series.

If you enjoyed this book and would like to share it with your friends, we have many resources for doing so. Just visit http://www.AmberSchamel.com and click on the Fan Resources page. You'll find free downloads of book banners, desktop wallpapers, a sample chapter of my books, and all kinds of fun stuff! You can even get your name on the Fan Hall of Fame by leaving me a comment!

If you don't already know me, I would love to meet you! Here's where you can find me:
Facebook: www.facebook.com/AuthorAmberSchamel
Twitter: @AmberSchamel
Pintrest: www.pintrest.com/AmberDSchamel
or on www.AmberSchamel.com

Chapter One

Circa 20 A.D.

The spring sun rose warm and clear over the Sea of

Galilee. Aaliyah bustled about in the small kitchen of their

villa. She had already been up for several hours preparing

for the Passover meal that evening. Despite the work, it

was one of her favorite nights of the year.

Footsteps sounded as her husband shuffled sleepily

into the kitchen. He lifted his hands above his head,

stretching his tall frame.

"Good morning, husband." She smiled at him,

suppressing her urge of mischief. "Did the sun creep up on you today?"

"I didn't sleep well," he grumbled as he dipped his hands into the bucket and splashed water on his scowling face.

Aaliyah scraped some fruit and porridge onto a plate for him. "You tossed and turned all night; I dodged several blows from you." She offered him his food, but when he reached out, she held it back. "Tell me, Tyrus, have you taken to beating your good wife in your sleep?"

"Perhaps if I did, she would behave during the day." Tyrus smiled softly and jerked the plate out of her grasp.

Aaliyah laughed under her breath. "Perhaps."

Picking up the bowl of dough she'd been mixing, she followed him into the dining room and sat across from him. As Tyrus ate, she studied him with a fond eye. He was still as handsome as the day she'd first seen him. His hair and full beard were dark as the midnight sky and his skin was tanned as evidence of his work ethic. His brown eyes were lively and ambitious; looking into them gave her the feeling that there were exciting new worlds he was waiting to conquer. His tall frame looked cramped sitting at the little table with his legs folded beneath him. Redness dabbed the nostrils of his distinct nose, the tell-tale sign, he was tired.

"What disturbed your sleep, my husband?"

Tyrus glanced up at her before replying. "Dreams."

Aaliyah's brow furrowed. "Dreams? What kind of dreams?"

He shoved his empty plate toward her and stood. "Never mind them now. Passover is tonight, and we've much work to do. The caravan I sent to Jerusalem is returning today, and I must inventory the merchandise before my patrons show up to buy them all. I'll bring our lamb in later." He turned and left the room before she could ask more. The courtyard gate slammed closed behind him.

Aaliyah bit her lip. His reservation seemed odd. Why would he not tell her of his dreams? Something about his manner gave her an uneasy feeling.

Sounds from the next room distracted her thoughts. The closing of the gate awoke their son, and the quick pitter-patter of feet sounded upon the tiled floor. Aaliyah crept through the courtyard and peeked into his room. Malon was sitting on the floor attempting to lace his sandals. His little pink tongue poked out as his chubby hands concentrated on the laces. Her heart warmed with a deep happiness as she watched him.

"Good morning, my son."

Malon's concentration was unbroken, and he continued

fumbling with the laces until he managed to put his shoes on. He jumped up, but when he did, the knot he had formed around his calf came undone and the laces fell down around his ankles.

"Aww. Imah, I just can't do it right."

"It's alright; I'll help you," Aaliyah giggled.

She winked at him as she knelt to tie the laces. He returned her gesture with a hard blink.

When his shoes were fitly tied, Malon jumped up and bounded across the courtyard, headed for the gate. He stood on his tip-toes, reaching for the latch.

"Where are you going, Malon?"

"With Abba."

"Don't you want some breakfast first?"

Malon's eyes swept around the courtyard as if searching for a hidden trap that would keep him away from his father. "Can I go with Abba after?"

"Yes, after breakfast you can go to the shop with Abba."

Malon followed her into the kitchen and plopped down on an overturned bucket. He gobbled down his breakfast as Aaliyah ran her hand through his thick, dark hair. "Don't eat too quickly. You don't want to choke on your food."

Malon's stubby hands extended the plate as his big brown eyes pleaded with her. "I'm finished now," he managed through a mouthful of food. "Can I go with Abba?"

Setting down the plate, Aaliyah took him by the hand, and together they walked across the courtyard and out into the road. The streets of Capernaum were busy with people rushing from shop to shop gathering the needed supplies for Passover. They crossed the street into the market and waved to their long-time friends, Simon and Andrew, as the brothers brought in the night's catch. The bleating of the lambs just herded into the marketplace added to the bustle and noise.

Aaliyah and Malon approached their family's shop. Kish, Tyrus' apprentice, was bent over stocking one of the displays.

"Shalom, Kish. Where's Abba?" Malon grinned.

"Aw, he's over paying the tribute for the shipment that just came in. Help me sort these figs and he'll be over just as soon as he's finished. We've got lots of work to do today."

A commotion from a nearby house drew Aaliyah's attention.

"No! Have mercy! Please husband, mercy!"

A man was dragging a woman, apparently his wife, out of the house and down the street toward the synagogue. "Silence you insolent whore. How dare you...and in my own house! No, woman! You deserve what is coming to you."

The woman struggled trying to free herself of his iron grasp and her screeching faded as they disappeared down the street.

Out of the corner of her eye, Aaliyah noticed Tyrus standing beside her. His jaw was clenched and his eyes narrow.

"You look a little pale, Aaliyah. Does this scene—" he turned and looked intently at her. "—bother you?"

Chapter Two

Aaliyah slapped the bread dough on the counter and kneaded violently. Tyrus' comment still rang in her ears. What did he mean by that? She had opened her mouth to ask him, but he walked away to inspect the wares. She heaved a sigh, determined to shrug it off and concentrate on the task before her.

A lot went into preparing the Passover supper. Last week, she had used up the last of the leaven so that the house could be cleansed for this special night. She prepared the dough for the unleavened bread, mixed, kneaded and formed it. Using a long wooden paddle, she placed the bread in the stone oven. Wiping her hands on her skirt, she turned around and surveyed the bitter herbs laying on the table at the center of the room. A small breeze wafted through the lattice window providing slight relief from the heat.

Tyrus entered the kitchen with a chunk of raw meat in his grasp. "Here's the lamb, Aaliyah. Where do you want me to put it?"

"Here." She replied pointing to a large bowl on the opposite end of the table. Tyrus laid the meat in the bowl and rinsed his hands in the basin. Aaliyah looked around as she began chopping the herbs.

"Where's Malon?"

"He's outside. Rabbi Ben-Simon came by and Malon is talking his ear off." He chuckled. "That boy has your tongue."

Her lips curled into a half smile as she shook her head at his sarcasm.

"Oh!" Aaliyah looked down. Her finger was gushing dark metallic blood. "I must have cut myself again. Tyrus, won't you hand me that towel?"

He tossed it to her with a hint of concern in his eyes. "Woman, you really need to be more careful. I don't care for blood in my food. It violates our kosher laws."

She flashed him a smile for his attempt at humor. He stepped closer, and examined her wound.

"That's a pretty deep cut."

"I'll be alright. It doesn't hurt much. You'd best get back with Malon."

Tyrus took her hand in his and looked closer at the cut. When he did, the sleeve of her tunic fell back exposing her forearm. His brow darkened.

"What is that?" He asked referring to a deep purple spot on her arm.

Aaliyah stared at it for a moment. It was ugly, circular and almost looked like a bruise. "I don't know, I must have bruised it, but I haven't noticed it until now."

Her husband let go of her hand and searched her face for a short moment. "I knew you were clumsy when I married you, Aaliyah, but you're not that clumsy. Are you well? You're hurting yourself all too often."

"I know. I've just been in such a hurry trying to get everything ready for tonight that I haven't been attentive."

"If you need help, I can arrange it. My sister could come to stay and help us if you need her."

"No, it's not too much. I'll be fine. Thank you, Tyrus."

He lingered for a moment longer before he left the house.

Aaliyah wrapped her finger in a strip of cloth and continued preparing the Passover meal. She was exhausted by the time she was done, but everything was prepared by sundown.

The smells of roasted lamb and freshly baked bread brought back memories of times passed when she had been as young as Malon, staring at the same foods, gathered round the table with her brothers and sister.

Setting the last bowl on the table, she sat down across from her husband.

"My son, why is this night different from all other nights?" Tyrus asked Malon.

Malon's brow wrinkled and the dimple on his left cheek appeared. "Because it's Passover?"

"That's right, my son. Do you know what the Passover is?"

A smile lit up the boy's face. He knew the story of Moses precisely. "When Moses led our fathers out of Egypt."

Even though the answer wasn't exactly correct, Tyrus' chest swelled with pride. "Well, just before that. You remember the part of the story when the plagues tormented Egypt?"

"Yes, Abba."

"Do you remember the tenth plague?"

Malon shook his head.

"The tenth plague is when the angel of death passed over all the land of Egypt taking the life of every first born in the land.

"Does that mean I would die, Abba?"

"No, my son. Adonai provided a way for the Israelites to escape that plague. Moses told them that if they would kill a lamb, like we did earlier today, and put its blood on the doorposts of their houses, the angel would pass over them and they would all be safe. Then they ate a special meal, like this one, before starting on their journey to the Promised Land. Today we eat this meal in remembrance of our deliverance from Egypt and in anticipation of our coming deliverance when the Messiah shall come and lead us out."

"What's a Messiah, Abba?"

"The Messiah is the one that has been promised to us by the prophets. Isaiah, David and many other prophets have foretold His coming. He will be God, come down to us in human flesh, to redeem us and deliver us again."

Aaliyah's pulse quickened. She loved hearing Tyrus speak of the Messiah. Thinking of how close His coming must be always sent shivers down her spine, and Tyrus' passion only added to the effect. She wondered if—perhaps in her lifetime—she would see the Messiah.

"When will the Messiah come, Abba? Will I get to see Him when He comes?" Malon curled his feet up underneath him to sit up taller as he looked wide-eyed across the table.

"We don't know when He will come, and we don't know what His name will be, but I do hope that if He comes in your lifetime, you will see Him and follow Him as one of His disciples."

Malon wrinkled his nose and sat back on his heels. "But, if we don't know His name, or when He will come, how will we know who He is? How will we know Him when He finally comes?"

A wide grin spread across Tyrus' face as it beamed with pride in his six year old son. "That's a good question, my son. The prophets have left us many clues as to who this man will be. He will be born from a virgin, and He will be born in Bethlehem. The Messiah will be a prophet who will tell the secrets of men's hearts, for this is the sign of God. He will be a healer, and He will speak boldly in His teachings; there are many other things, but I will teach you more as you get older."

"Abba, what's a virgin?"

Tyrus' mouth twisted. Apparently that wasn't a question he was expecting. Aaliyah cleared her throat.

"I think that's enough questions for tonight. The food is getting cold, and I am starved. Aren't you, Malon?"

"Sure am, Imah. And this honey looks yummy."

Tyrus and Aaliyah exchanged a glance of relief. Tyrus lifted the cup of wine above his head and began the ritual prayer.

"Blessed are You, Lord our God, King of the universe for the vine and the fruit of the vine, for the produce of the field. The offspring of Your servant David may you speedily cause to flourish, and enhance his pride through Your salvation, for we hope for Your salvation all day long. Open the eyes of thy people to see him when he comes. Blessed are You, Lord our God, King of the universe."

*****

Aaliyah woke with a start. The sun was already up and she'd somehow overslept. This had been happening often as of late. Scrambling out of bed, she staggered across the courtyard to the wash basin in the kitchen. She splashed water on her face, rubbed her hands together and scrubbed at the reddish-purple splotches on her arms in brisk motions. There were increasing numbers of those splotches, but she tried to hide them from Tyrus. They would upset him.

With a sigh, she gripped the side of the table. Tyrus had been short tempered with her lately, and she still wondered why. Several things about his behavior seemed odd to her. Like the remark he'd made about the adulteress in the street, and these dreams, they had been disturbing his sleep for several weeks, but he still refused to tell her what they were. She could also tell that he was wondering if HaShem had shut her womb. Their son was six years of age and she had not conceived since he was born.

A certain fear gripped her heart at these thoughts. When she had married Tyrus, she was deeply in love with him, but to Tyrus it was only a contract. Something that had been arranged by their parents long ago and he was expected to fulfill. She had hoped that once she proved she was a good and faithful wife and had bore him a son that his feelings would change, but if she were barren, and could only bare him one son. If these splotches on her skin were serious. Would all her chances at winning his love be lost?

Shaking these thoughts aside, she pulled back her long, dark hair and began preparing the morning meal. As she poured the cakes before the fire, the door creaked behind her and Tyrus' heavy gait entered the room.

"Good morning, husband." She said without turning.

"You're awake. Are you feeling better today?"

Aaliyah wiped her hands on her apron. "I think so. I'm sorry I am late."

Tyrus tossed something onto the table and shuffled to

the basin. "How long until breakfast is ready?"

"Sit down and have some milk. The cakes will be done by the time you've finished your cup."

Tyrus poured some milk from the pitcher and disappeared into the dining room.

When the cakes were done, Aaliyah scooped them onto a plate and hurried to join her husband in the next room.

"Here you are, Tyrus."

Triumphantly, she set the plate of cakes on the table. When Tyrus glanced up, his face filled with alarm.

"Your face...what's wrong with your face?"

Fear clenched her heart as her hand flew to her cheeks. "My face?" She frantically patted her chin felt a series of large bumps. The terrified look on Tyrus' face was like none she'd seen before; she must look awful.

"Aaliyah, go to the bathing room. Don't touch anything. I'll bring the physician." He shook his head with concern. "I should not have waited this long."

"Tyrus..."

"Go, woman, and don't touch anything."

Malon appeared at the doorway. "Imah, what's wrong?"

She turned to him, but Tyrus catapulted out of his seat and scooped Malon up in his arms, holding the boy's head against his chest. His eyes met hers with a firm gaze.

"Aaliyah, go to the bathing room. Malon and I will bring the physician. For now, don't touch anything."

Aaliyah numbly obeyed. She leaned against the cold stone wall, and waited for the physician to arrive and pronounce her fate. Her heart filled with dread as her mind sorted through the facts. Leprosy was the most feared disease in Israel, and all of the signs, the splotches, her lack of feeling in her fingers, and now the bumps all evidenced that it was indeed this disease. Leprosy was incurable, and highly contagious. If indeed the physician thought it to be leprosy, she would be banished from her home and synagogue. They would exile her to the leper colony far outside the city to waste away until she died.

"Adonai, please, do not curse thy handmaid." Her prayer was hardly a whisper, but she didn't know what else to say. She curled up on the floor and waited.

Chapter Three

It seemed like hours had passed before she heard footsteps in the courtyard. Tyrus appeared with the physician, but Malon was not with him.

"The first thing I noticed is that she cuts or hurts herself more often than usual. Then red and purple splotches appeared on her arms, and today, bumps broke out on her face."

"Aaliyah, please look at me." The physician stepped closer, but kept a safe distance.

She raised her head and looked at him. His eyes were filled with compassion, but his mouth was firm. "Can I see the spots on your arms?"

She pushed her sleeves up to her elbows exposing the

hideous sores. The physician's lips pressed together.

"It's what I thought it was, isn't it?"

"I'm afraid so, Tyrus. Your wife is infected with Leprosy. Do you have any idea as to how she has contracted this disease?"

Tyrus shook his head.

"Aaliyah, please think. We need to know if you contracted this disease from somewhere or someone so that we can protect your family from also falling victim the disease."

"I — I don't know." Aaliyah was so stunned she could hardly speak and her hands trembled.

The physician nodded and turned to Tyrus. "Tracing the origin of the disease is almost impossible. It can be months, even years between coming in contact with the disease and becoming infected by it. I'm afraid there's nothing I can do."

"Thank you, Judah. I appreciate you coming down so quickly."

Judah patted him on the shoulder before leaving the house.

Once they were alone, Tyrus looked at Aaliyah. She quivered, curled up on the tile floor, her head tucked against her knees.

"What have you done, Aaliyah?"

She frowned as she looked up at him. "Done? Tyrus, what are you saying?"

"Do not play innocent with me. Your sins have found you out. Confess them now, and perhaps HaShem will see fit to heal you."

"My sins?"

"Yes, your sins. I shrugged off my dreams because I didn't believe you would do it, but Adonai has exposed you. He has done so to give you the chance to confess and be cleansed. Confess it now—please Aaliyah—confess it and I will forgive and beg Adonai for mercy."

His words pierced deep. She might as well have been bitten by an adder. So this is what he thought of her? That she was a sinner so filthy that Adonai would curse her with the most dreaded disease in the land? His condemnation was worse than the disease itself.

"I have nothing to confess. I have lived my life according to the law since my youth."

Tyrus stepped back and crossed his arms. "So that's how you're going to be? This time your conceit will do you in."

"Tyrus, how can you say these things? You have known me almost my entire life. You must know in your heart this can't be..."

"God does not punish the innocent, Aaliyah!" His shout

silenced her. Calming himself, he stepped back again. "You are dead to me. I will keep Malon away from this house until it has been thoroughly purged. If you have any care at all for our son, you will leave and never return. I will not risk Malon's life. If I see you anywhere near this house, I..."

He didn't finish, he just stared at her for a moment. Then, turning abruptly, he strode out of the house.

"Tyrus, please. Tyrus. Tyrus!" Her useless screams collapsed into broken sobs as she sat alone in the silent house. "Adonai, I don't understand. Why have you done this to me?"

Finally mustering her strength, Aaliyah rose and gathered a few things from the house. Her gaze fell upon Malon's little wooden archers. He loved them and played with them for hours.

She fingered the smooth wood. "Tyrus will probably burn everything in this house."

She picked up three of the soldiers and slipped them into her basket. These would be all that she had to remember Malon by. Kneeling before her wooden chest, she rummaged through the clothing looking for her woolen tunic. Her hand fell upon something hard, so she pulled it out of the folds of fabric. It was the golden bracelet that Tyrus had given her upon their betrothal. It was a smooth gold bangle with pomegranates carved into it. It still shimmered in the light as she held it in her hands.

She gripped the side of the chest to steady herself as surges of emotion flowed through her body. She clenched the bangle in her fist and raised her hand to throw it out the casement, but as all the good memories of their years together came flooding in, tears welled up in her eyes and she placed the bracelet on her wrist. It sparkled with brilliance and purity in the sunlight that streamed through the window.

"Surely it must all be a dream. A terrible dream." She pressed her hands to her eyes and hot tears overflowed from the pressure. "Oh, wake up. Wake up."

She rocked back and forth on her heels for several moments. When she again looked up, she saw a small white dove sitting on the open casement. It coed at her then spread its wings and flew away.

Taking a deep breath, Aaliyah stood and wrapped a black cloak around her shoulders. Grasping the handle of the basket, she trudged toward the courtyard gate. Pausing for a moment, her hand lingered on the threshold. She remembered the day that Tyrus had first brought her to this house. He had softly taken her hand in his and led her inside saying, "I built this house with my own two hands. In the years to come, we will make it a joyful place filled with laughing children." That would never be.

Aaliyah took an uneven breath as she turned. She took one last look at the house that had been her happy home only moments ago. Then, flipping the hood over her head to hide her tainted face as best she could, she passed through that door for what would without a doubt be the last time.

Chapter Four

Aaliyah kept her head down as she ambled through
the city streets. There was only one place she could go.
Outside of the city, nestled in the rocky hills of Galilee,
was a leper colony. A commune of outcasts who were
deemed 'unclean' by society. There they lived out their
miserable existence together until the infection and disease
finally freed them from misery. It was a life of solitude,
poverty and pain. This was Aaliyah's fate.

Moving aside so a cart could pass, she continued
winding her way between houses toward the city gate.

"Aaliyah, shalom." A happy, familiar voice called out
as she passed the marketplace. Hannah had been her
dearest friend since childhood. They had grown up

together and were blessed enough to live close to each other even after their marriages. Hannah was making her way across the street toward her.

Aaliyah squeezed her eyes shut. Everything was different now. She didn't want to utter the word, but she had no choice. The law—and her friend's safety—demanded it.

"Unclean." The word came almost as a wail and she wasn't sure if Hannah understood it.

Hannah hesitated, and then continued toward her with cautious steps. "Aaliyah? What's wrong?"

"No, Hannah. Do not come any closer. I am unclean." The words sent sharp pains through her stomach, but if Hannah came too close, she too might suffer the same fate; and Aaliyah could not let that happen.

Her shouts started to attract attention, and some crossed over to the other side of the street to pass.

Hannah stood still, her brow knitted together. "Aaliyah, what are you speaking of?"

"I am cursed. Adonai has made me unclean."

Her friend stared at her for a long moment. She must see the hideousness of Aaliyah's features. "Tyrus has banished you?"

Aaliyah nodded as her hands again began quivering.

"Where will you go?" Hannah's deep brown eyes were

filled with sorrow and compassion.

"The Colony. Where else could I go?" An awkward pause followed. "Goodbye, my friend." Aaliyah turned and hurried down the street toward the gate. She had to get out of the city as quickly as possible. The pain was more than she could bear.

When she finally reached the outcropping of the leper colony, Aaliyah was exhausted. The residents of the colony looked strangely at her as she wandered into the village. She halted near the center of the commune and looked around unsure of what to do next.

The village was made up of a series of small, multi-member houses made of crude mud-brick and sandstone. There was a cistern near the center which was the only thing about the village that resembled a normal city. There were people all around. Some just crouched in corners moaning in pain, others tried to care for those worse than themselves. Still others were busy grinding wheat that some charitable person had sent to the colony.

An old woman suddenly appeared at her side. Her face was withered, and her nose was sunken from the disease, but she spoke with a kind voice. "Ah, you're a young one. Poor child. Come this way, a bed just opened up in the woman's quarter."

The woman shuffled toward the north side of the

village. Hesitantly, Aaliyah followed. The woman ducked inside one of the little huts. Her high, nasally voice echoed off the stone walls. "In here, child. It's not much, but it will give you a place to sleep at night."

Ducking inside, it took a moment for Aaliyah's eyes to adjust to the darkness of the enclosed shelter. It was a small room with a straw pallet beside each of the four walls, and another in the center. Two of the beds were occupied by sleeping women, and the other two were rumpled as evidence that they were also in use. There was only one empty pallet, and the old woman's rag-wrapped hand pointed to it.

"You're fortunate that a bed opened up for you. Most have to sleep out in the open air for the first few weeks of residency."

Aaliyah set her basket of belongings in the corner.

"You must have been a rich one too. Not many here have any belongings of their own."

"My husband is a merchant in Capernaum. He was going to burn everything in the house after I left, so I took a few things with me." She looked around the room again, still wary of these new surroundings.

"That one is mine." The woman said pointing to the pile of blankets in the center. "So I'll be here to keep you company. Life in the colony can be difficult the first few weeks."

"And after that?" Aaliyah asked as she raised an eyebrow.

The woman chuckled. "Well, after that I imagine you get used to being lonely and unclean."

Aaliyah imagined what this woman would have looked like before the disease. She must have been lively with rosy cheeks and a plump build with a gleeful laugh. But now, her frame was frail and her face sunken, but her laugh still exuded happiness, and her friendship was a rainbow in her stormy sky.

"How long have you been here?"

"Me? Child, I've been here for six years, two-hundred twenty three days and five hours." She chuckled again. "No, truthfully I don't know how long I've been here. I don't even know what today is."

"Surely you must have a guess."

The woman's face sobered. "I guess it's been about fifteen years. My husband died shortly before I came down with the disease, and they ran me off at the first signs. There's a potent fear of leprosy in this country, you know."

Aaliyah snorted. "Yes, I know."

The woman cocked her head and eyed her intently. "What's your name, child?"

"Aaliyah."

She nodded thoughtfully. "Nice to meet you. My name is Meira."

Meira. That was a perfect name for her. Before Malon was born, she had chosen that name in the case that he was a girl. The name meant "one who gives light" and right now Meira was the only light in her life.

*****

Aaliyah opened her eyes and looked around. Everything in her house was just as she had left it the night before. Tyrus was still sleeping by her side, his heavy breathing the only sound in the stillness of the morning. She slipped out of bed and peaked into Malon's chamber. He was sleeping soundly, his face as peaceful as a cherub's. She breathed a sigh of relief and slumped back against the doorway. It must have all been a dream. The leprosy, Tyrus' anger, the colony, Meira, all just a dream.

She made her way to the wash basin. The sun was coming up and she would need to make breakfast for her family. She dipped her hands into the cool water and splashed it on her face. Her eyelids re-opened, refreshing drops clinging to her lashes, when she caught sight of her reflection in the basin. Her face was hideous, tainted and sunken like Meira's. Terror surged through her body, pulsating through her arms, legs, and chest until it finally escaped from her mouth in a shrill cry of panic.

Chapter Five

Aaliyah sat upright in the darkness, her breath coming in sharp gasps and her brow damp with sweat. All of the night sounds were unfamiliar, wheezy snores, howling wind, and pain filled moans in the distance. She whimpered like a lost and frightened child.

"Nightmares are normal for the first few weeks in the colony." Meira's high, nasal voice brought remembrance of the previous day and where she was. "The question is which part is the nightmare? Your dream or what you wake up in?" The old woman's shadowy figure lay down again and nestled into her blanket.

Aaliyah's hand touched her face; she felt her cheeks, nose, forehead and chin. Her face was the same, except for those large, ugly bumps below her lip. She rested back on the straw, the mixed emotions of sorrow, relief, and pain making their way down her cheeks in an incessant stream.

She could not sleep for the rest of the night. Lying awake on the straw pallet rubbing Malon's wooden soldiers between her fingers, thoughts raced through her mind. She wondered where Tyrus was, what he had told Malon, if Tyrus would re-marry and replace her in their lives. She wondered how, after all this time, Tyrus could think that she had sinned in such a way that Adonai would brand her as unclean, banishing her forever.

She finally fell back asleep after dawn, just in time for Meira to get up and start moving about. The straw rustled under her as she turned and pulled the blanket over her head. Meira was kind enough to let her sleep.

Several hours later, Aaliyah woke again. She sat up and leaned against the stone wall that was already growing warm with heat. It must be late in the afternoon for the stones to be so warm. She curled up and hugged her knees to her chest. She'd woken up in a nightmare she never thought possible.

"Adonai, why have you done this to me? What have I done to deserve this?" Her whisper was hoarse from exhaustion.

She paused, waiting for an answer, but the only sound was a fly that buzzed in the corner.

"Will you be silent? Will you not answer me? "Her eyes stung with the pressure of hot tears trying to escape.

Only stillness.

Aaliyah curled up under the blanket again, tried to sleep, and forget about her sorrow.

Several days passed this same way. Sleeping was filled with nightmares, and waking hours were worse, haunted by thoughts of Tyrus and Malon, sunken faces and angry words. She was falling into a bottomless, dark hole. Deeper and deeper into a unfathomable pit of obscurity.

One morning, just as dawn broke the sky, she was lying awake on her pallet when a hand touched her shoulder. She turned to see Meira's sunken face smiling at her.

"Come on, child. Time to get up."

Aaliyah shook her head. "Why?"

"You can't be morose forever. Come, child, there's much to do."

Meira got up and started toward the door. She pulled back the flap and sunlight streamed in. "Come on, Aaliyah."

She ducked outside, then the curtain fell and all was dark again. Aaliyah sighed and lay her head on the straw. "Surely she won't make me go out. I only want to curl up and die here in this grotto." She snorted. "Isn't that what

Tyrus is counting on?"

"Aaliyah, child, hurry along," came the voice from outside.

With a huff, she threw aside her blanket, strapped on her sandals and obeyed Meira's call.

She squinted from the brightness of the sunlight she'd not seen for more than a week. Holding her hand up as a shield, she strained to catch sight of where Meira had gone.

"Over here, child."

Turning, she saw Meira holding a water bucket.

"Fill this with fresh water and bring it back, if you would. I trust you can remember where the cistern is?" she gave a slight giggle, probably amused at Aaliyah's groggy expression.

"I can find the middle of the village, but if I don't come back, look for me on my pallet."

She grasped the rope handle of the bucket and started toward the cistern. As her eyes adjusted to the light, she could see that it was a beautiful and clear day. The blue skies contrasted with the warm rays of the sun that made a drifting haze over the golden sands. It would be hot today.

There were two other people at the cistern when she got there. The first was a middle-aged woman and the other was a man that wasn't much older than his companion. As Aaliyah approached, she heard their conversation.

"Nephtalim?" The woman asked sweetly."How long have we been here?"

"It must be about three years by now."

"Three years." The woman shook her head. "It's hard to believe it's been so long. That means Talia is of marriageable age now. I do hope Alcazar is looking after her."

"Don't worry, my love. Our son is a man of duty. He will take good care of Talia and find her a good husband."

"How I wish we could see them. I miss them terribly."

The man put his arm around his wife. "I know, but it just isn't possible."

He glanced up when Aaliyah reached the cistern. Then taking the bucket in one hand and grasping his wife's in his other, the two ambled off toward the huts.

Aaliyah's mouth twitched as she watched them go. How blessed they were to be together. What she would give to have Tyrus truly love her as this man did his wife...but it would never be. Tyrus had banished her and made it clear that he would never look upon her again.

She ignored the nagging pain and filled the bucket.

When she found Meira, the old woman was gathering sticks from beneath a few straggly trees. "Thank you, child. How much time it will save me to have an assistant. You know, I'm not as young as I used to be. I've been praying for someone to take my place before I go. Come, child."

Meira led the way, weaving in and out of the little huts until at last she stopped.

"How do you ever tell the difference between the huts? They all look the same to me."

Meira laughed. "You'll catch on by and by. When you know the people who live inside each one, it's easier to remember."

There was a small fire pit outside the hut with a boiling pot hanging over it. Meira started arranging her sticks in the circle of rocks below the pot.

"Inside this hut lives woman named Lael and her son. Lael is the daughter of a Levite, but she married into the tribe of Judah. Sometime later, she and her son fell sick with leprosy. All of the people thought it was Adonai punishing her for marrying outside of the Levitical line. That is when she came here."

Soon the little fire was burning. Aaliyah emptied the contents of her bucket into the boiling pot then they sat down to wait.

"It shouldn't take long to heat the water; the day is already growing warm." Aaliyah wiped her brow. "What are we going to do?"

"The warm water will soothe and cleanse their sores. I'm afraid they don't have much longer, but I do what I can to keep them as comfortable as possible until then."

Aaliyah bit her lip. She had forgotten that death would be a daily part of life here. Her stomach churned at the thought. *I wonder if Tyrus knows what it's like here. He probably doesn't care anyway. I'm cursed and deserve to live this way for the wicked life I've led.*

Looking down at her hands, she realized that she'd been clenching them. She quickly released them and wiped her sweaty palms on her knees. "Where do you get food and other things you need?"

Meira smiled. "That you shall discover shortly, child." She ladled out a little water. "Would you be so kind as to see if the water is warm yet? I've lost most of the feeling in my hands."

Aaliyah dipped a finger into the ladle the old woman held out to her. "It's warm."

"Good. Then let's go inside." She poured some of the water into a basin and ducked inside the hut. Aaliyah followed reluctantly behind her.

The hut looked the same as all the others, but was filled with oppressive heat, and there was a stench unlike any she'd ever experienced that made her stomach lurch. The woman was lying on a pallet of straw, tossing and writhing in pain. She was much younger than Aaliyah had expected, probably younger than herself.

There was a basket sitting by the door. Meira pulled several rags from it and stooped before the young girl. "I'm here, Lael." She stroked her brow before dipping a rag into the basin and dabbing at the sores that covered the girl's face. "Is Chaim asleep?"

The girl managed a few pained words. "Yes, he's finally so exhausted that he fell asleep. Thank you, Meira. HaShem bless you."

"Her son hasn't slept in several days," Meira said when Aaliyah's gaze met hers. "Hopefully he sleeps a while. There's some salve in that basket, would you get it for me, child?"

Aaliyah found the clay jar amidst the rags and set it next to the girl. Just then a babe started wailing. Turning, she saw a baby boy, no older than eighteen months lying in a wooden box that was crudely padded by a blanket.

"The poor child. He'll need his sores soothed as well. Aaliyah, you see what I'm doing here, do you think you can do the same for the baby?"

Aaliyah swallowed hard. "I...I think so."

Meira smiled in approval. "Refresh the water in the basin please then bring the child over here so you don't have to walk across the room to use the basin."

Aaliyah grasped the sides of the bowl and the sordid water sloshed inside it as she carried it to the door. She tossed out the stinking water and refilled it with fresh water from the boiler pot.

Reentering the little hut, she was again hit with the strange odor, but summoning her courage—and holding her breath—she set the basin down and approached the wooden box. The child was still crying in pain, but she couldn't see his face because it was hidden by the blanket. When she pulled the blanket away, it revealed a poor helpless creature whose disease was more advanced than its mother's. It hardly looked human anymore.

Tears of sympathy filled her eyes as she picked up the child with gentle hands. "Shhh, it's alright. I'll help you, sweetheart."

She set him beside his mother, dipped the tattered rag into the warm basin of water and gently dabbed the sores on his face like Meira had done to Lael. At first, he bawled even louder, the sores must have been tender to the touch. As she applied the salve, he calmed to soft whimpers.

She fought back tears as she lay him back in the box and kissed the only patch of skin on his arm that was not infested with sores. She felt a soft touch on her arm.

"Come, child. It's time to go." Meira gathered up the

soiled rags and slipped out of the door.

Aaliyah knelt beside Lael and touched her shoulder. "We'll be back tomorrow." She gave her a soft smile and followed Meira outside.

Meira had removed the boiling pot and was now stooped before the little fire burning the soiled rags. Aaliyah stood beside her with folded arms.

"The baby got it first, didn't he?"

"He did."

Aaliyah let out an uneven breath. Such love a mother has for her son. Lael could have let him die alone, but instead would risk her own life to care for her child. She thought of her own son, and whispered a prayer thanking HaShem for sparing him from this wretched disease.

"They don't have much longer, do they?"

"No, child. Not long at all."

When the rags were sufficiently ash, Meira stood and faced Aaliyah. "You asked where we get the food and supplies from. Now, my child, you shall see. Come."

Chapter Six

Meira led the way as they wove in and out among the little huts and walked down the rocky hillside toward the city. When they were about half way between Capernaum and the colony, Meira deviated from the path and headed for a group of scraggily rocks.

"Meira, where are you going?"

The old woman glanced over her shoulder and raised an eyebrow, but continued without a word.

"If you're tired, can't we rest somewhere else? That looks like the perfect place to find a cobra."

Meira kept walking, not hearing a word she said.

"Meira," Aaliyah called in a harsh whisper. Her nerves tingled as the distance between them grew larger. Seeing that her friend wouldn't be deterred, she followed at a distance.

Meira halted about fifty yards from the outcropping and pointed her tattered finger. Her eyes followed her direction, and she saw three women and a man loading bundles from a cart onto a portable sled. Aaliyah strained to recognize their forms.

"Hmm," Meira commented thoughtfully. "There's usually only the good rabbi and his wife and daughter. Someone else is with them today."

"The Rabbi?"

"Yes, child. Rabbi Ben-Yaakov comes once a week and brings supplies and food for the colony. We have to take it from here back to the village because he cannot make himself unclean by coming himself. The woman next to him is his wife, the other girl holding the mule is his daughter, but I don't recognize the third woman."

The third woman had her back to them as she bent down to pick up a bundle from the cart and transferred it to the sled. When she turned around, Aaliyah's eyes widened, and her jaw dropped.

"Hannah?"

The rabbi's wife noticed them standing in the distance and waved. The third woman also spotted them and walked a few steps closer. The rabbi's wife touched her arm and gave her a cautioning glance, but the woman came closer still.

As the space between them narrowed, the woman's features became clear.

"Hannah? What are you doing here?"

"Aaliyah. HaShem be praised. I prayed I could see you again."

Hannah stopped about seven feet from where Aaliyah stood.

"It's so good to see your face."

Aaliyah turned away. "My face is tainted."

Hannah shook her head. "That doesn't matter to me. I have known you since I was a child, and I know you never could have sinned so terribly as to bring this upon yourself. We never know Adonai's thoughts, but surely He has a plan in this."

There was a short pause. Aaliyah tried to speak, but when she opened her mouth, no sound emerged. She swallowed hard and shut in the tears welling in her eyes.

"Here, I brought something for you."

Hannah pulled a shell from her pocket and held it out to her.

"Simon found this shell in one of his nets the other day. It was so rare and beautiful that he saved it for me. I asked him to carve some teeth into it so that it could be used as a comb. I thought you might have need of it."

Being careful not to touch her, Aaliyah took the gift from Hannah and rubbed her fingers on its smooth surface. "Thank you, my friend, and thank your husband for me as well."

"Hannah, we must go now." The rabbi's wife called.

"Yes, coming," she said looking over her shoulder. "Goodbye, dear friend. I will come again, I promise."

Aaliyah nodded and Hannah turned to join the others as they led the cart down the hillside back to Capernaum.

Meira walked over and examined the goods on the sled. "Oh, how kind of the Rabbi, he brought us honeycomb. Lael will enjoy that. Come, child, we must get this sled to the colony and put away all the stores before it gets dark."

*****

The next morning, Meira and Aaliyah rose and made their way to Lael's hut. Everything was the same as the day before. Lael tossed and turned on her pallet, and the child slept in his makeshift crib. They nursed the mother first, hoping to let Chaim sleep as long as possible.

The girl's voice sounded weaker than yesterday. "Thank you, Meira, I feel much better now. Chaim should wake soon. He slept all night. It's the first good rest he's had in weeks."

A strange look crossed Meira's face, but vanished before the woman noticed.

"That's good, child."

Lael took a wheezing breath. "Did I ever tell you how long my husband and I prayed for a son?"

"No, child. I don't think you have."

"We had one daughter, but when she was an infant, I had taken her with me to the market and when my back was turned she ran out into the street chasing a stray dog." Her voice choked and became hardly more than a whisper. "She was run over by a band of Roman soldiers. It was my fault. I did not care for her well enough."

Meira wrapped her arms around the trembling girl.

"I figured HaShem was punishing me for that when He wouldn't give us more children, but I begged and prayed for two years that Adonai would give me another chance. He finally did."

"No one could ever say that you didn't care enough for Chaim. You are the most faithful mother I have ever met, child."

The girl wept in Meira's arms for several minutes. Finally, she fell asleep exhausted from her tears.

Meira held one finger over her lips, gently laid the girl

down and tip-toed out of the hut. Aaliyah followed closely behind her.

"We will come check on her again this afternoon." She said when they reached fresh air. "In the mean time, we need to distribute the food rations to each hut."

Meira had a gift of keeping herself busy, and she had extended that gift to Aaliyah as well. She was grateful for her old friend and for the work too. The busyness kept her mind off of the painful memories and haunting questions. It was only when she tried to rest that they all came back to her. This resulted in fitful sleep and continued nightmares.

"I'm feeling weary. I think I'll lie down after this," Aaliyah said as she distributed the last bundle of food.

"I'm sorry, child, but would you mind coming with me to check on Lael first? I have a feeling that I will need your help."

"Of course, I nearly forgot. We didn't bathe Chaim this morning. We'll have to soothe his sores now."

"I hope so," Meira mumbled under her breath.

"What do you mean?" Aaliyah said frowning.

The old woman glanced up at the sinking sun. "It's getting late. Let's hurry."

Meira had a knack for avoiding questions, but Aaliyah let it rest and followed her to Lael's hut. The stench inside the little chamber was worse than it had been earlier. Aaliyah pressed the back of her hand over her nostrils and remained that way for several minutes before her nose adjusted enough to breathe.

Lael sat up when they came in. "Is it afternoon already?"

"My child, it is nearly night. I'm sorry we took so long. There was much to do today."

The girl suddenly became uneasy. She glanced toward her son's bed. "Chaim hasn't woken yet. He's been sleeping for ever so long."

Aaliyah's fingers suddenly became colder than a Roman's heart and a tingle crept up and down her spine. Her eyes fell upon the small form lying beneath the blanket in the box crib. Her legs carried her to the little bed, and she stiffly bent and picked up the child. Immediately she knew. The body was growing stiff, and the child didn't wake. A strong odor emanated from the swaddled infant.

Raising her gaze, the mother's eyes locked on hers. Lael glanced at Meira then back to Aaliyah. She grimaced and her head shook slightly.

Aaliyah's chin trembled. "I'm...I'm so sorry."

"No. No!"

The girl leapt from where she'd been sitting and

groped at the bundle in Aaliyah's arms.

"Chaim. Chaim, wake up. Wake up!"

Her hands flew to her face and she clawed at her insipid cheeks.

"My son, my son. Oh Chaim!"

Falling to her knees, her voice became a blood curdling wail as she grasped at the child's body. She fell at Aaliyah's feet and curled up like a wilted flower.

Meira tried to wrap her arms around her, but she swung her fists.

"Leave me! Leave me here to die."

The old woman winced, but she stepped back and bowed her head, waiting for the fit of grief to pass.

Aaliyah stood helplessly, clutching the baby tightly to her chest as silent tears streamed down her cheeks.

This cannot be happening. She slowly lifted the blanket from the baby's face, but dropped it again as soon as she saw what was left of it underneath. *I knew he would go quickly, but I didn't think it would be this soon.*

Lael had quieted, her frame quivering on the exposed floor. Meira came forward again.

"Put him back in the box." She whispered. Then she knelt and wrapped her arms around the poor mother's shoulders.

"It's not your fault, child. You did all you could. You're

a devoted mother. No one can doubt that, child."

Aaliyah set the corpse into its place and staggered toward the door. The tears welling in her eyes blurred her vision as she stumbled in the direction of her hut. When she finally reached it, she tripped over a woman that was already in bed. Falling onto her pallet, she buried her face in her hands, salty tears gliding between her fingers.

She dug her hands beneath her pallet and pulled out the only thing she had of Malon's, his wooden archers. She held them gently in her hands as images of her son flashed in her memory. What if he had contracted the disease as well? What would Tyrus do with him if he did? She laid there for several hours, different scenarios plodding through her mind, until she could bare it no longer. She had to know what had happened to her baby boy. She tiptoed to the door and slipped out into the dark night.

Chapter Seven

Aaliyah struggled to find her way in the darkness as her puffy eyes gradually adjusted to the dimness of the night. The moon was hidden behind a cloud and offered little light. Her fists tightened at her side as her determined steps carried her toward Capernaum.

By the time she had made her way down the rocky hillside to the city, the sun was beginning to rise. She paused in a group of trees and watched the gate. Soon, it opened and the first of the merchants, and travelers began to trickle through.

Where would Malon be? Where would Tyrus have taken him? Aaliyah's brow creased as she thought. She glanced up at the rising sun; she would have to leave soon before it was light enough for people to recognize her and her disease.

"I should have thought to bring my cloak. That would have been a great help right about now."

Another merchant passed through the gate.

"I'll move along the alley toward our house. Maybe he's cleansed it already. That route will take me past the market without all the crowds."

Glancing in both directions, she saw the gate was clear. Taking a deep breath and exhaling through her mouth, she then walked toward the gate. She made an effort to make her strides confident; she would be less conspicuous that way.

Turning down the first street that went behind the market into the more prominent neighborhood, she heard people bustling about in the marketplace. A glance ahead alerted her that someone was coming. She waited for them to get just close enough then stooped as if she'd dropped something. Groping through the sand, she waited for them to pass her in her hunched position before rising and continuing on her way.

Her steps carried her further down the alley until she would be directly across from her husband's shop. She ventured toward the market, finding an imperceptible spot behind a large tree. Leaning against its rough bark, she searched the market.

There, inspecting goods coming in on one of the carts was Tyrus. His dark tresses clung to his forehead as sweat trickled down his strong brow. A strange feeling washed over her. She wanted to run to him, for him to take her in his arms and tell her everything would be alright. But she also wanted to turn and run away from him as quickly as she could. Never to see him again.

She rested her head against the trunk of the tree and took a deep breath. Looking around again, she searched desperately for Malon. Perhaps he had come to the shop with his father. Her fingers toyed with the tree bark as she watched. Their voices were faint from across the square, but she could tell Tyrus was negotiating with the trader.

"Abba, look at this."

Malon appeared from the other side of the cart holding a long string of gold with purple stones. He held it up before his father.

"Can we buy it for Imah?"

Aaliyah whimpered and her hand covered her mouth as she fought back tears so she could watch her little boy clearly. Tyrus fingered the necklace and a pained expression came over his face.

"Imah won't be needing it, son. Please put it back."

Malon's smile faded and his head bowed, but he

obediently walked back around the cart.

Aaliyah felt a tug on her tunic.

"Excuse me, excuse me, Miss."

Turning, she saw a small girl who had unwarily approached her. When the child saw her face, a look of terror came over her delicate features and her mouth opened releasing a shrill scream.

Immediately, all eyes turned to her, and the girl's father came from around the corner. His eyes quickly assessed the situation and widened with alarm. Grabbing the child's arm, he jerked her away from Aaliyah's reach.

"Unclean. This woman is unclean!"

Fear gripped Aaliyah as she glanced around at all the angry stares and fearful faces. Then her eyes met Tyrus'. For a moment, she was paralyzed as a hundred messages were conveyed through a glance.

Why have I come here? How could I have endangered others this way? They'll kill me now. Her only other thought was *run*. Run as fast as she could away from this place and never come back.

The adrenaline in her veins spurred her into action and soon she was sprinting toward the gate. Sounds of footsteps behind her confirmed her fear; they would pursue her and stone her for coming into the city. It was bringing sin amongst the people, not to mention endangering them; therefore it was strictly forbidden.

Just as she reached the gate, a stone struck her back causing her to fall. Dust enveloped her and she could taste the sand that filled her mouth. She turned over and scrambled backward when she saw her pursuers approaching her. Her breath and heart accelerated. This would be the end, and there would be no way to hide it from Malon.

The crowd was in an uproar. How dare a leper come back into the city? It was against the law, and these laws were made quite clear. With shouts, they grasped stones, and waved their arms as their eyes flashed.

A rabbi came forward and the crowd hushed. He stepped close to her and looked down his pointy nose. "Why have you come into the city?"

Aaliyah didn't know what to say. She tried to speak, but all that came out was a stammer even she couldn't understand.

"You are unclean. Don't you know it is forbidden for the unclean to approach the city?"

Short gasps came from Aaliyah's throat as she nodded her head.

The rabbi wrinkled his nose and spit at her feet. "Stone this unclean woman. She is possessed with a devil."

Again the roars of the crowd ensued. Aaliyah curled

up, waiting for the blows to begin.

"Wait! Stop."

Tyrus' deep voice pierced through the air and caused every head to turn upon him. He stared at her, his lips pressed tightly together.

"Be gone, woman. Don't ever come back."

"Tyrus...I..."

"Get out. If you are caught near here again, I will stone you myself."

There was a silent pause as Aaliyah absorbed the words just spoken to her by the man she called her husband. Slowly, she rose and turned toward the gate. Taking one step, and then another, and another, she made her way out of the city.

She didn't look back until she was halfway up the hillside. Tyrus was still visible as he stood at the gate, watching her disappear amongst the crags. It was then that her spirit broke and deep sobs rose to the surface, jolting her entire body. Curling her head into her chest, she covered it with her arms.

When she finally raised her head again, she concealed her face with her hands. "Am I so ugly now that I terrify children? I pray Malon didn't see me like this." She broke into sobs again as her hatred lashed at the city. "I hate you. I hate you all." She covered her face again.

When Aaliyah finally made it back to the colony, she stumbled into her hut and frantically rummaged through the basket of her belongings. She pulled out one of her tunics and tore the expensive fabric into a long strip. She wrapped the fabric around her head and covered her face with the homemade veil leaving only her eyes exposed. Leaning back, she finally felt safe behind her mask. Her breath warmed her face as she started to relax and her breathing steadied. Her head rested on the straw and sleep engulfed her.

*****

She must have slept for a long time, because when she woke the sun was rising and Meira was shaking her shoulder.

"Wake up, child; it's time for Chaim's burial."

Aaliyah sat up quickly and her veil fell into her lap. She picked it up again and wrapped it around her head.

Meira's head cocked and her brow rutted. "What are you doing?"

"I'm putting on my veil."

"Why do you need a veil?"

"Why? Meira your vision must be fading with your age. I am hideous and tainted. Once I was lovely and young, but now my face frightens small children."

Meira's eyes widened as understanding crossed her features. "You went near the town, didn't you?"

Aaliyah bowed her head and a tinge of shame made her cheeks heat. "I had to see what happened to Malon."

"My child, we cannot allow the actions of others to dictate ours. I don't know what happened to you down there, and I don't need to know. Here, we're family." She extended her hand and removed the veil from Aaliyah's face. "We don't need to keep secrets, or hide anything. We're in this together. Do you think you look worse than I? No. No. Here, it is not our looks, but our hearts that determine our beauty."

A tear slipped down Aaliyah's cheek, but Meira quickly brushed it away with her mothering hand and gave her a tender smile.

"Lael needs us now. The best way to heal our hurt is to care about someone else's."

Aaliyah nodded and followed Meira out of the hut to the burial grounds.

A small gathering of people, all in tattered robes, huddled around a small but deep hole in the grassy hillside. The babe had been wrapped up tightly in his blanket and anointed with smelly herbs before being placed in the little wooden box that had been his crib. His mother was crumpled beside it, her eyes swollen from constant weeping and her voice hoarse from the eerie, sorrowful wails that emanated from deep within her heart.

Aaliyah glanced at Meira before kneeling next to Lael and placing her hand on her shoulder. The frail frame quivered beneath her hand like an overripe fig about to drop from its branch.

The others gathered around began to shift nervously. Looking up, Aaliyah saw two figures climbing the hillside to the burial site. As the figures came into view, she could see that one was the rabbi, but the other man was a stranger to her. The group of lepers migrated to the farther side of the grave, leaving room for the clean ones to approach.

The man who accompanied the rabbi stared at Lael and the box beside her. His mouth twisted and he began to weep. He turned and walked a few paces away clenching and unclenching his fists. At last he turned back to the group.

"I wish to see my son."

The rabbi's eyebrows rose, his glance questioning the man's decision.

"I want to see him."

"He may not be recognizable, Gad."

The man pressed his eyes shut. "Please, let me see my

son."

The rabbi nodded at Meira who bent and gently lifted the blanket exposing the child's sunken face. When his eyes fell upon the child, the poor man whirled around and vomited into a nearby bush.

"Are you sure you want to go through with this?" Rabbi Ben-Yaakov placed a hand on his shoulder.

He wiped his mouth with the back of his hand. "I can do it. I just need a moment."

The rabbi nodded and stepped back to his place at the head of the grave. A long moment passed before the man again approached. He inhaled steadily and nodded at the rabbi.

Aaliyah helped Lael to her feet and held her up as Rabbi Ben-Yaakov began reciting a psalm. Lael's red eyes met her husband's and held them for a long moment before her strength failed and she again slumped into Aaliyah's arms.

"Chaim is a beloved son of Gad Ben-Aish, his faithful wife Lael, and of Adonai. Though his life was short on this earth, we know that he is resting with his fathers and we look forward to the day that we may join him in paradise."

The rabbi nodded at two men who lowered the little box into the grave.

"May HaShem grow exalted and sanctified in the world

that He created as He willed. May He give reign to His kingship in your lifetimes and in your days, and in the lifetimes of the entire Family of Israel, swiftly and soon."

The rabbi paused. Aaliyah's lips mechanically joined those gathered. "May His Great Name be blessed forever and ever."

"Blessed, praised, glorified, exalted, extolled, mighty, upraised, and lauded be the Name of the Holy One, beyond any blessing and song, praise and consolation that are uttered in the world. May there be abundant peace from Heaven and life upon us and upon all Israel. He who makes peace in His heights, may He make peace, upon us and upon all Israel. Amen."

"Amen."

The echo of the mourners' voices hung in the air until it was broken by the cry of the father. He tore his clothes, dropped to his knees and covered his head in dust.

The rabbi stooped and picked up a handful of earth. "Blessed is the Judge of Truth."

With this final prayer, the dirt streamed out of his hands and onto the casket below. The other mourners did the same, one after the other until there was only a few left at the graveside. The two men that had lowered the casket finished filling in the hole.

Aaliyah stood with Lael until it was all finished. Then,

gently turning her shoulders, she guided her toward the colony.

When they passed her husband, who was still sitting in the dirt, she stopped. Again, her eyes held his for a long moment.

"I did all I could. Please say it wasn't my fault this time." Her voice was so hoarse, Aaliyah wasn't sure the man understood it.

"No. You are more faithful than I. You have been faithful unto death, and I am a coward. I abandoned Chaim when he needed me most. You have every reason to be ashamed of me, but I do love you."

Again there was silence, but even Aaliyah could see that there was something passed between them that words could never express, and it prodded her heart.

After guiding Lael back to her hut and leaving her resting under Meira's care, she paced several yards outside of the colony. She slumped behind a thick palm tree and rested her head against the trunk as silent tears streamed down her cheeks.

"What I would give for Tyrus to say those words to me." A broken sob escaped her lips. "Lord, why could I never make him love me?"

She wasn't good enough to be loved when she was whole. There was no chance he would ever love her now.

Taking a deep breath she swiped at her eyes. "No. It doesn't matter anymore. I don't want him to love me. I am ashamed of him. He is a coward. He judges too quickly and he sees only the evil. I am done with him. For the rest of my life."

Chapter Eight

The rising of the sun brought no surprise when they found Lael's lifeless body lying beside her son's grave. The rituals and preparations from the day before were again repeated and a message was sent to Rabbi Ben-Yaakov.

Funerals were a regular part of life in the leper colony, and soon Aaliyah became accustomed to them. She busied herself by helping with all of the arrangements and ceremonial preparations for each poor soul that was finally freed from their diseased captivity. This task hardened her in a way that nothing else could.

She often imagined what her own funeral would look like. Hannah would be there, of course, but would Tyrus even bother to come? Would Malon know that she had died? Or perhaps he thought she already had. Thousands of times she replayed in her mind what Tyrus had said to her, and wondered what lies he had fed Malon about her. Her hatred for Tyrus—and mankind in general—deepened during those years.

As time went on, Aaliyah's rich tunic faded, and so did the memories. But the pain was still a constant ache in her chest. Hannah continued visiting her once a week when the rabbi's family brought the stores of food and supplies.

Aaliyah could not tell how the disease had progressed on her, for she didn't dare look at her reflection. She could see that her hands were becoming tattered and began to resemble melted wax with the fingers curling inward. This made it harder to do her duties. She wrapped them in old shards of cloth for protection, but mostly so she wouldn't have to look at them.

Besides Hannah's visits, Meira was the only light in Aaliyah's dark world of pain and hatred. Meira's disease progressed as well, and more and more Aaliyah had to help her with things she had done herself for years. Yet her cheery spirit never failed, and she was always the first one awake and ready for work.

"I wish I could still taste the food you make me, Aaliyah." Her knobby hands wrapped around a small stick she was using to stir the fire.

Aaliyah smiled faintly. "Perhaps it is better you don't. It doesn't matter what I make; you tell me how much you like it."

Meira chuckled and leaned back against a rock. "You are a blessing to me, child. It's like the Lord gave me the daughter I never had."

"Then perhaps I should take to calling you mother instead of Meira." Aaliyah handed her a plate of vegetables and matzo.

"I think I would like that, my child."

A warm smile passed between them as they both sat quietly. The sounds of the night seemed comforting. The chirping crickets, the hoots of Tawny Owls, and the crackling of the fire made a symphony just for them.

"Mother," the sound of that word on her lips made Aaliyah smile. "What do you miss most about normal life?"

"My child, that has been quite a long time ago." She shook her head, and her eyes seemed far away. "There are so many things. I miss my husband's laugh, the warm feeling of his hand in mine, the sound of my three sons playing together in the street. Still, I think what I miss most is going to the synagogue and hearing the Torah."

"I just don't understand why HaShem allows these things to happen."

"No mortal can answer that, child. Adonai's ways are not our ways; our thoughts are not His thoughts, as the prophet Isaiah said."

"How can you have such faith and trust when...when Adonai has left you this way?"

"Left me?" Meira tipped her head back and a laugh emerged. "My child, Adonai has never left me. If He had left me, I wouldn't have you."

Meira squeezed her shoulder. "HaShem is still with us. He will not leave us comfortless. Just hold onto that. Never get angry with Adonai for what you don't yet understand. Being angry at Adonai is the worst thing one could do. Aaliyah, my child, never question the clouds, because they're only bringing the life-giving rain."

Meira rubbed her back. "You'll make it through this, Aaliyah. Even your name attests to that."

"My name?"

"Yes, child. You're name means to 'overcome' or to 'rise above'. You will rise above your pain and circumstance. Adonai will help you."

Aaliyah picked up a stick laying in the dirt and twirled it between her fingers. "Do you...do you think Adonai is punishing me?"

"For what, child?"

Aaliyah bit her lip. "I don't know. Tyrus thinks I've

done something awful and HaShem is cursing me for it, but I have followed the law since my youth. I have been among the most devout Hebrew women."

Meira bent forward and held Aaliyah's gaze. "So you are sure you've done no wrong?"

"Yes, I'm sure."

"Then don't let Tyrus take that away from you. Adonai sends us trials, but He doesn't punish the innocent. Remember the story of Job? He had many trials, all terrible ones, but it wasn't because he was sinful. If the Lord has given you a peace in your conscience, don't let go of that."

Aaliyah let out a breath she didn't know she'd been holding. A feeling of relief flooded her soul, evidenced by a smile on her lips.

"Thank you, Meira. I'll sleep much better tonight."

The old woman gave her a sly grin. "Well then daughter, off to bed with you."

Aaliyah bent down and gave the old woman a kiss on her forehead and slipped off to bed.

*****

The sun was shining in her eyes when Aaliyah awoke the next morning. Though the day was clear, it was cold. She pulled her blanket up to her chin and shuddered beneath it.

Glancing at Meira's cot, she saw that she was still asleep.

Ha, I'll finally rise before her for once. Aaliyah thought with a smirk. *I'll get the fire burning and warm it up in here.*

Pulling her aging cloak over her shoulders, she tip-toed toward the hearth. Throwing some kindling on the hot coals soon revived the flames and its warmth began to fill the little hut.

She slipped outside to draw water and took a deep breath of crisp morning air. Her step was lighter than it had been yesterday. Her talk with Meira the night before had lifted a burden from her shoulders and it was as if the sun was shining new in her heart again. She began humming a tune as she swung the water bucket in time with her steps.

When she made it back to the hut, she put some water on to boil and ground the corn for their morning porridge. The other sleepers soon began to rouse, and shuffled around in the little hut.

When another woman sat down beside Aaliyah, she glanced at Meira who still slept soundly on her pallet.

"Meira must be getting tired in her old age. She's usually up before us all."

The woman beside her nodded and stirred the water in

the pot. "The smell of porridge will wake her, I'm sure."

Aaliyah poured the golden granules of corn into the pot of boiling water and stirred. The porridge soon thickened and she scooped some out into each of the wooden bowls.

"Alright, Meira. You've slept long enough, Mother. Come and get your porridge."

She scooped porridge into three other bowls that were held out to her.

"There won't be any left if you don't come now."

The old woman still didn't stir, so Aaliyah walked across the hut and tapped her on the shoulder.

"Alright, old Mother, you can't be that tired. Time to rise. There's much to do."

She gently held her shoulder and turned her over, but the old woman's head just flopped limply to the side. It was then that she realized how cold Meira's shoulder was, and how stiff she seemed to be.

"Meira? Mother, please wake up."

Fear gripped her heart so that she could hardly breathe.

"Meira? Meira." She shook her roughly, but the woman's eyes still wouldn't open. "Mother, please. This is a cruel trick. Wake up."

Holding her breath, she lowered her head to the

woman's chest and listened.

There was nothing. No steady beat. Only cool stiffness.

"No. No, please, Meira. Don't leave me. Mother please come back."

Broken sobs shook her slight frame. Everything around her faded away. All she could see, all she could think of was this poor, dear woman. A lone candle glowing in her darkness as her only light. Now, that light was snuffed out. Aaliyah was alone. Left to herself in a bleak world.

Chapter Nine

Circa 30 A.D.

"There goes Aaliyah. Off to see about the man's funeral I suppose. The poor thing, she hardly says a word anymore. Do you remember, Bracha, how she was when we first came here?"

A middle-aged woman looked up from drawing water and watched Aaliyah enter the hut of the deceased. "That I do, sister. Before Meira died, she was a pleasant sort. Anymore she is hardly more than a walking post. So hard, cold and quiet all the time. I pray I never get that way."

"Oh, Bracha, be kind. Poor Aaliyah has been through much from what I hear. I heard that her husband banished her from his home, forever forcing her to leave her young son and everything she ever knew." The woman sat down on the ledge of the cistern and leaned toward her sister. "Rumor has it that Adonai is punishing her for being unfaithful to her husband."

"Is that so? Well, she deserves it then. I guess taking care of the dead bodies is a job that suits her."

*****

As Aaliyah ducked into the hut, she could hear two women laughing as they sat at the cistern.

What could they possibly have to laugh at? She wondered as she covered her nose against the stench of death. *Don't they understand that their turn isn't far away? I'll soon bury their bodies, just as I did Meira's.* She shook her head as she stared at the body lying on the table. *If only Tyrus knew what he has sentenced me to. It might break even his hardened heart.*

Tying a napkin around her face, she began the work of preparing the body for burial.

"I can't imagine what You will think of him at the judgment, dear Lord. Condemning one's innocent wife to a leper colony." She shook her head. "I certainly wouldn't want to be him."

Near the end of the day, Aaliyah made her way to the outcropping where she would meet the rabbi and his family bringing the food and supplies. She watched from a distance as Hannah and the rabbi's family transferred all of the goods from the cart to the sled.

"Go ahead without me. I'll be along after while." Hannah's sweet voice drifted across the field that separated her and Aaliyah. "I wish to speak with my friend."

"Please use caution, Hannah. Your continued friendship toward Aaliyah is charitable, but don't endanger yourself."

Aaliyah winced. Being talked about in third person is bad enough, but the thought that Hannah's friendship had become merely 'charitable' was almost more than she could bear. It was true that Hannah's visits had become shorter, in fact, last week she hadn't come at all.

She stood helplessly as the rabbi's family rumbled away in the cart leaving Hannah near the sled of supplies.

Hannah turned in Aaliyah's direction, waiting for her to approach. Taking a deep breath, she moved forward, resolved that she would only stay a few moments. There was work to do and she didn't want to be an inconvenience; as 'charitable' as it may be for Hannah. She stopped when she came within six feet of her. "Shalom,

Hannah."

A smile like she'd never seen before spread across Hannah's face. "Hello, my friend. I have much to tell you."

Aaliyah's heart fluttered. What news could she have? What could possibly make her so glad?

"I've not seen you this happy since your marriage was arranged with Simon."

"Oh, Aaliyah, never have I had the cause to be so happy. I will tell you everything, but first, how does it go with you, my friend."

She snorted. "How does it go with me? My husband banished me to hell on earth and believes that I have been unfaithful to him. I am plagued with the most dreaded disease of my day, and I tend to the bodies killed off by the same. Please, Hannah, I would rather talk of something else."

Hannah pursed her lips together. "I'm sorry, Aaliyah. Your husband has no right to accuse you of such things."

"Yes, well, perhaps his sins will one day find him out and he too will be banished to a life of misery."

Hannah shifted. "I pray not."

Aaliyah knew that such a thought should bring a feeling of regret or sympathy. A sincere hope that such a thing would never befall her husband. But instead, she almost wished it upon him.

"He and Malon are doing well." She chuckled. "Malon has learned to be quite a salesman. Just yesterday I was near their shop and he came running out to show me a tapestry that had just arrived from Jerusalem. After pointing out every intricate detail, he asked me if I wanted to buy it, and I was shocked to find that I did. He told me he would get me a good price on it if I came back this afternoon. Tyrus says he sells nearly half of their volume now."

Aaliyah bowed her head. It had been nearly ten years since she'd last seen her son. The pain of him growing up without her was still keen, and she felt short of breath.

"Please, can we change the subject now?" Her question was barely a whisper.

Hannah stood silently for a moment.

"Aaliyah, what if you had the chance to be well again?"

"What are you talking about, Hannah? No one has ever been healed of leprosy."

"Because there was no one with the power to do it. Aaliyah, for so long we have awaited the coming of the Messiah, and now He is finally here. That is what I have been so anxious to tell you."

Aaliyah's brow rose involuntarily. "Hannah, you know as well as I that 'Messiahs' are as plentiful under Roman rule as eggs under a setting hen. What makes you think this 'Messiah' is really the One?"

Hannah sat down on a rock and folded her hands in her lap as if to contain her excitement. "Well, my mother had taken ill. She was very, very sick with the fever. We thought for sure she would die. She was thrashing around like a mad woman, hallucinating and crying out. That's why I wasn't able to come here with the rabbi last week."

"Hannah, I'm so sorry."

"Just listen. A few days ago, Simon and Andrew were bringing in the nets, after fishing all night, when a man came along and stood on the shore watching them. When Simon noticed him standing there, the man smiled and said to him 'follow me.' Simon told me he knew there was something different about this man, so he and his brother both dropped their nets and followed him."

"Hannah, dear, your husband is a wonderful man, but he has been known to be rash at times..."

"I'm not finished." Hannah shook a playful finger at Aaliyah before she continued her story. "Do you remember the crazy man at the synagogue with the spirit on him?"

Aaliyah nodded. That man had been there for many years. He stayed near the synagogue tormenting anyone that passed by that way to enter the house of Adonai.

"Anyway, when they went into the synagogue, the

possessed man was there. He screamed out at the man saying 'leave us alone. What do you have to do with us, Jesus of Nazareth? Do you come to destroy us? We know you are the Holy One of God.' Simon said he was afraid, until Jesus spoke. He said 'Hold your peace, and come out of him.' The spirit threw the man on the ground with a great shriek, but then he was still. Simon helped him up off the ground, and the man was as sane as you or I. I saw him with my own eyes. After they were done at the synagogue, they came to our house. And the tormented man sat like any other and ate with us."

"The mad man with the spirit?"

"Yes. When I saw what was done I said to Simon, 'We must ask him to heal my mother.' For she'd gotten worse and I was afraid that she would die that very night if Jesus didn't heal her. So we went to the Teacher and we asked Him to heal my mother. He went into the room where she was and stood over her. 'Demon, I say unto thee: be gone. Let the woman be well,' he said. Oh, Aaliyah, if you could have seen it. My mother's eyes opened, her chills left her and she rose up out of bed for the first time in weeks and helped serve supper to all of them."

Aaliyah's eyes searched hers. "All you've said is true?"

"That and more. Word spread quickly about the mad man and my mother's healing. Soon our house was surrounded by people begging Jesus to heal their sick. Aaliyah, this must be the Messiah. I saw limbs restored, blinded eyes receive their sight, and demons flee from Him with only one word from His lips." Hannah touched her arm. "Aaliyah, this man can heal you."

Aaliyah recoiled at her touch. No one had touched her since Meira had died. Her head was spinning, what if this was, in fact, the Messiah? What if He could heal her?

"Where is this Jesus of Nazareth?"

"At present he is staying at my house, but He intends to travel to Tiberius tomorrow. He goes round the region of Galilee; there's no telling when He will be near here again. You must come with me, Aaliyah. Come with me now. Jesus will touch you, and you can be well."

Tears welled in Aaliyah's eyes; her heart was torn. This was the first ray of hope that she'd had in many years. The chance of her being made well had never before crossed her mind. But the fear of Tyrus, of the villagers, of being seen with her disfigured face overpowered her. The expression on the child she had terrified the last time she went near the town flashed before her memory. She shook her head.

"No, Hannah. I cannot go to Capernaum. If I were to show my tainted face there again, they would all surely stone me."

"Not if you are made well. Aaliyah, please come with me." Hannah reached for her hand, but Aaliyah jerked away from her grasp.

"No. I can't."

Aaliyah turned and stumbled away, forgetting about the food and supplies. Tears blurred her vision and her hands trembled as she tried to make her way back to the colony. Her foot caught on a shred of her hem and she fell to the ground. Her knees and bandaged palms broke her fall. She stared down at her battered hands and noticed little tears dropping down onto them. She had not felt the tears streaming down her face.

She turned over and sat in the dust. Raising her hands, she patted her disfigured face.

"How can I show my ugly face in Capernaum again? They will kill me."

You're going to die anyway.

She clutched her ears trying to ignore the voice in her head. "No, I can't go."

Jesus is your only hope. If He would heal you, you could see Malon again.

"Tyrus would never let me come home, not even if I was cleansed. It is not because of the sickness that he hates me. He despises me because he believes I've been unfaithful to him. He would never take me back."

Suddenly realizing how odd it would seem that she was talking to herself, she looked around. She could see a pair of travelers coming up the path. Scrambling to her feet, she looked around for a place to hide. Not far off was a large fig tree. She darted toward it and hid behind its gnarly trunk.

The distant voices of the travelers became audible.

"Yes, Jesus of Nazareth is his name."

"Nazareth? Can anything good come out of Nazareth?"

"There was a man who was lame from birth. His legs were curled up in a disgusting manner, but when Jesus prayed for him, I saw the legs unravel before my eyes."

The gravel on the path crunched as the man stopped in his tracks. "Before your own eyes? You saw this first hand?"

"Yes, and many other miracles. You have to come see for yourself. Come on."

Aaliyah peeked out from behind the tree as the two travelers hurried on their way.

Maybe Hannah was right. Maybe Jesus could heal me. But how could I ever get to Him? Surely they wouldn't allow a leper anywhere close to him. I just don't see any possible way.

Chapter Ten

Aaliyah leaned against the edge of the table.

Preparing a body for interment was grueling work. It was sweltering hot inside the little hut and the air was so fetid she could hardly breathe even through the napkin that covered her nose and mouth.

Her eyes fell to the bowl of water beside her. She could see her reflection on the surface of the water. There were wrinkles around her eyes that had not been there the last time she'd seen her reflection, and dark, puffy bags lingered beneath them. She had not slept in three days, and her appearance confirmed it. Every night she would lie awake as thoughts of Jesus of Nazareth troubled her.

Hesitantly, she raised her hands and untied the napkin

that covered her nose and mouth. Lowering it, she held her breath as she unveiled her tainted face. The odd formation of bumps on her chin had spread, now encircling her mouth. The right side of her face looked droopy and inhuman. Her heart sank at the sight.

"There is no possible way I could go into the city like this. Just a glimpse in my direction would give me away."

Her stomach suddenly twisted and she ducked outside into the fresh air. She leaned against the cool stone wall as she waited for the nausea to pass.

What if you had the chance to be well again?

If you were healed, you could see Malon.

Conflicting thoughts wrestled inside her head.

They'll kill me if they catch a glimpse of me.

You're going to die anyway. What do you have to lose?

They can't kill you if you're healed. What if Jesus would heal you?

"Aaliyah?"

She shook herself and turned. One of the newest residents stood a few feet away.

"Yes?"

"You have a visitor. She is waiting for you a few paces down the path."

"A visitor?"

The man nodded.

"Thank you. I'll see them directly."

The man shrugged and walked away.

"No one ever visits the leper colony. Who could possibly be here to see me?" She wondered aloud as she made her way through the village. A sudden dagger of fear struck her heart. "Malon? Oh Adonai, please, let no harm befall Malon."

Her pace quickened with the rate of her heart as she advanced a few strides down the path and saw a woman sitting beside the road waiting.

"Hannah?"

The woman jumped up and brushed off her tunic. "Aaliyah, it's good to see you."

Aaliyah placed a hand on her fluttering stomach. "Is everything alright?"

"Yes, everything is fine."

"Malon is well?"

An understanding smile spread over Hannah's face. "Yes, Malon, Tyrus, everyone is well. I'm sorry if I gave you a fright."

The breath Aaliyah had been holding escaped through her lips. She shifted her feet and folded her arms. "Then...why have you come?"

Hannah's eyes dropped to the ground. "I know you said you won't come to Capernaum, but Jesus will be returning tomorrow morning for the last time before he leaves to Jerusalem for the feast. We don't know when He'll be back."

Aaliyah shook her head. "Hannah, I told you before. I'd be stoned before I made it anywhere close to Jesus. And even if I did, his disciples would never allow me close enough to him to be healed."

"Simon is one of his disciples. He knows you; he would not restrain you."

"I appreciate your concern, Hannah, but there is simply no way." She turned and paced a few steps away. "Did you know I entered the town once before?"

"No," Hannah replied.

"I did. They chased me to the gate and raised stones to cast at me when Tyrus intervened. He swore that if I came near the city again, he would kill me like a deranged dog."

The angry faces of the mob flashed before her eyes along with images of fists clenched around jagged rocks. She turned and faced her friend.

"I simply cannot go."

Hannah pursed her lips together and exhaled. "Well, if you change your mind, the Master will be teaching near the gate in the morning."

With one last, hesitant glance at Aaliyah, Hannah turned and walked back to the town.

*****

Aaliyah's pallet of straw might as well have been a bed of rocks and needles. She tossed and turned all night, her thoughts bickering with her heart.

"Augh! How am I supposed to live like this?" She threw off her blanket and stared at the black ceiling.

"If I don't go, I will spend the rest of my life wondering if I could have been healed, if I might have returned to my family, if I might see Malon again. But if I go...Adonai, my heart is gripped by fear."

She rolled over on her side and curled her knees to her chest. "Adonai, what am I supposed to do?"

She lay there, trying to sort through her thoughts for several long moments. When finally the fog in her mind lifted, she could see one thing clearly.

"I cannot live knowing I passed up a chance to return to my son." She rose and peered out of the doorway. Evidence of the sun was appearing on the horizon. "If I am to go, I will have to go early to be sure I can get close enough to reach Him."

She turned and looked around the dim room. "I will take my cloak. If I wear it low, and keep my face hidden, perhaps I can get close enough before they suspect me.

That will give me one advantage I didn't have the last time."

Once again looking out the doorway, she took an uneven breath. Then, summoning her courage, she snatched up her cloak and ducked out of the hut.

Chapter Eleven

Aaliyah's heart raced as she approached the city gate.

The sun was cresting the horizon, but already a large crowd was gathered along the main street, waiting to see this Carpenter from Nazareth. She could tell the time He would appear must be drawing nigh, for the crowd grew louder with each moment that passed.

As Aaliyah neared the crowd, she pulled her cloak over her head and pulled it down tight. She must hide her tainted face at all costs. She looked around for a place where the Master would pass. This was her one chance to be healed and she would not let it slip through her tattered fingers.

The sun beat down on her back and made her swelter

beneath the ragged black cloak. Keeping her head down, she noticed the shreds of costly fabric, which she once called her tunic, trailed along the dusty street. Tyrus had given her that tunic on their seventh anniversary. How long ago that was.

Many other people began to gather around, whispering excitedly and bumping into her. She struggled to keep her place near the street. Her breathing came in shallow huffs as she tried not to panic. Each bump and shove brought with it the risk of being exposed.

Suddenly a deep familiar voice boomed from behind her.

"Out of the way woman. Can't you see you're blocking the way of the cart?"

Aaliyah's heart stopped at the sound of his voice. In her effort to get close to where the Master would pass, she had unknowingly placed herself in the middle of an alleyway that entered the main street. She dared not look up and risk showing her disfigured face but she knew beyond doubt...that was *his* voice. She choked as she stepped aside. The merchant cart laden with wares rolled past her, its driver not even looking back. She stared after him, his wavy dark locks had grayed slightly, but there was no question; it was Tyrus. The man who had held her heart and future in his hands, and crushed them when he banished her from his sight.

She staggered as she fought back tears that formed from the vivid memories of the day that her husband dispossessed her...and the day he swore to stone her. Her chest constricted as her whole abdomen seemed to form into a tight knot.

How could he truly believe that she had done something so wrong that HaShem would curse her with this terrible disease? After all this time, after all they'd been through...she just couldn't understand. He knew her character better than anyone in the world. She had contended for his love since the day their parents had arranged the match. She still remembered being that young girl of eight, staring at the handsome merchant's son who — with a twinkle in his eye — presented some exotic toy to each child in the house. He may have been eight years older than her, but she didn't care. She had fallen in love with him then and had done everything in her power to please him, but it had not been enough.

The thoughts of her husband cooled her heart, and though the day was sweltering hot, she shivered. Doubt whispered in her ear. *Even if this Healer could help you; would He help you? He will probably despise you as do the rest of your people. This man will not help you. He will see through to the real person beneath the cloak. An ugly, tainted, bitter woman.*

Suddenly a pair of worn sandals stopped in front of her. The mob grew silent. The Master stood in front of her.

Aaliyah's hands trembled. She didn't dare look up, for anyone who saw her face would run her out of the city. What should she say? Here was the Healer standing in front of her and she couldn't bring herself to make the request she had longed for. She broke and crumpled to the ground in a puddle of tears.

The Master placed His hand on her head. "Why have you come to me?"

The sound of His voice sent a chill down her spine. Hannah had been right; there was something different about this man. She buried her face in her hands and tried to speak through her sobs. "My Lord, I am unworthy."

Jesus knelt before her, slid the cloak off her head and took her bandaged hands in His. A gasp rippled through the crowd of onlookers as Aaliyah's disfigured face was exposed. Aaliyah pressed her eyes shut and her heart dropped. Surely they would run her off now, or stone her for coming back into Capernaum. She waited for the eruption that was sure to ensue.

"Aaliyah,"

Her confused eyes met Jesus'. How did He know her name?

"You have come to ask me to heal your body, but there is a deeper illness that plagues you."

Jesus glanced in the direction where the merchant cart had trundled away just moments ago. Aaliyah understood what He meant. The bitterness she felt toward the man who rejected her was holding her heart captive worse than the disease that bound her flesh. Now, as she looked into the eyes of the Master, she could see that her heart was as ugly as her face because of the bitterness that had infected it. When her people had abandoned her, she had abandoned her God. As this realization rushed over her, tears began flowing from her eyes and her frail frame shook with emotion.

"My Lord, forgive my sin and heal my heart's disease that seeks my life."

In that moment, Aaliyah forgot about her deformed flesh and thought only of her deformed heart. Perhaps all the onlookers who stared at them could not understand what had passed between the Lord and His servant, but the Healer understood the true need of this outcast.

Jesus turned and held out His hand.

"Water."

Aaliyah then noticed Simon standing next to Jesus. He handed Jesus a goatskin he'd been carrying on his shoulder.

The Master unwrapped Aaliyah's hands and poured water over them. Then He looked at her as if He could see into her heart. "Go. You have been made clean. That which the Lord has made clean, will no man call defiled."

Jesus helped Aaliyah to her feet and an astonished gasp arose from the crowd. Everyone stared at her. Even the birds were silent for one brief moment as The Healer's hand held onto hers.

Chapter Twelve

Suddenly, someone began shouting, "Hosanna. Hosanna!"

That one voice spurred a pandemonium of shouts and chatter. Some shouted "Hosanna to the Son of David." Other voices jeered at the crowd. "Blasphemy. This is Blasphemy. This man heals by the power of Beelzebub."

At first, the fuss of the crowd confused her. She glanced at Simon who gave her a big grin, and her heart leapt to her throat. Her trembling hand found her face. It was smooth as silk, soft as flour.

Chickens squawked and darted for cover as Aaliyah ran to the well as quickly as her feet would carry her. She stumbled several times over the shreds of tunic that trailed the ground.

When she reached the well, she let down the gourd that served as a bucket and poured the water into a clay vase that was sitting on its edge. She peered inside the vase. The reflection made her heart skip a beat. Her face was as clear and smooth as it had been the day she was wed. She stared at herself for a moment then a smile spread across her face, narrowing her vision and sending a thrill of joy through her heart. She looked back toward the gate, but the Master was gone.

His words echoed in her heart; "That which the Lord has made clean, will no man call defiled." No man? Could that mean her husband also?

Aaliyah looked back at her reflection. She knew that her heart was now as beautiful and new as her face. The ache inside her was gone; replaced by a feeling of gratitude and joy she could not explain. The Healer had touched her, and she would never be the same.

Stepping back, she turned around in a slow circle as her eyes searched her surroundings. What should she do now? Should she seek out Tyrus?

"Aaliyah." Hannah ran up to her and threw her arms around her neck, nearly toppling her over. "Simon told me you came, and I see it's true. Here, let me look at you."

She placed her hands on Aaliyah's shoulders and

pulled back as she examined her face.

"You look as beautiful as you did on your wedding day." She kissed her friend's cheek. "I'm so happy for you. How do you feel?"

"I—I feel different." Her brows knitted together as she tried to explain. "I feel happy, but calm, yet still slightly confused."

Hannah nodded. "Jesus is different than anyone in the world, isn't He?"

"Yes. Where is He? I wanted to thank Him." Her eyes wandered past her friend, searching for any sign of Jesus.

"Gone, I'm afraid. He's started for Jerusalem. Simon ran back to tell me before catching up with Him."

Aaliyah's heart sank. "I wanted to see Him, to thank Him, and ask Him what I should do."

"What you should do? You go home of course." Hannah giggled at her friend's hesitancy.

"Hannah, Tyrus believes I have been unfaithful to him; my being healed doesn't change that. He won't accept me back."

"Are you still angry with him?"

"No. I'm not angry anymore. In fact, it surprises me that I want to go back, to be reconciled to him again. Moments ago I would have fought that. I'd only hoped I would get to see Malon again, perhaps be able to visit him.

But when Jesus spoke to me..."

Hannah nodded knowingly. "Meeting the Messiah changes a person, I know."

The Messiah? Yes, He had to be. No one else could have healed a leper.

Aaliyah lifted her hands but dropped them again by her sides. "I guess I feel helpless; I don't know what to do."

"Maybe if we could get a message to Tyrus, tell him that the Messiah has healed you, perhaps he would see the truth and consider taking you back again."

This sounded like a logical, if doubtful, plan. Aaliyah nodded. "I suppose that's where we should start. Maybe he would at least consent to let me see Malon. Will you try, Hannah? Will you get Simon to talk to him?"

Hannah's head cocked to the side. "I'm not sure when Simon will be back from Jerusalem, but I will try."

"Thank you. In the mean time, I return to the colony."

"The colony? My dear friend, why would you go back there? You're not a leper any longer. Jesus healed you."

Aaliyah gave a short laugh. "I know that better than anyone, Hannah, but there are people in the colony that need my help. Maybe I could convince them to come to Jesus. He could heal every single one."

"That He could, but what will you do?"

"There is plenty a healthy person can do around the

colony. Someone has to bring the supplies and food from Rabbi Ben-Yaakov."

Even though her nose wrinkled at the idea of her friend going back to the leprous village, Hannah nodded. "What if you get sick again?"

"Hannah, I have been healed. Adonai would not have healed me just to get the disease again. The more I think of it, the more sure I am that this is what I need to do. At least until your husband can speak with Tyrus."

"Then I guess your mind is made up, but always know that you have a place with me. I get lonely while Simon is gone."

Aaliyah wrapped her friend in a tight embrace. "Thank you."

As she turned and made her way back to the colony, a strange feeling came over her. Now she entered the village, not as a resident, but as an aide. She wondered at this feeling deep in her heart; it was a feeling she had not felt in ten years ...a longing. A longing to again see Tyrus' face, to hold his hand, look into his eyes and see a genuine love. Could that be possible? Tyrus had not loved her before; how could he possibly come to love her now? Yet the Messiah's words echoed inside her mind.

"That which the Lord has made clean, will no man call defiled."

The End.

Don't miss Book 2 in the Days of the

Messiah Series!

**Disease, extortion, and the beguiling lies of a false
messiah...which is most dangerous?
~Volume 2 The Messiah's Sign~**

Thank you for reading! We hope you enjoyed the journey.

If you enjoyed The Healer's Touch, please consider leaving a review on Amazon, Goodreads and your favorite sites. Telling your friends about the book is the best compliment you can give to an author.

You can contact the author and keep up with her new releases by connecting with her on the following links

Facebook: www.facebook.com/AuthorAmberSchamel

Twitter: @AmberSchamel

Pintrest: www.pintrest.com/AmberDSchamel

or on www.AmberSchamel.com

Printed in Great Britain
by Amazon